GET IN SHAPE, SNOOPY!

Peanuts® characters created
and drawn by Charles M. Schulz
Text by Linda Williams Aber
Background illustrations by Art and Kim Ellis

A GOLDEN BOOK • NEW YORK
Western Publishing Company, Inc., Racine, Wisconsin 53404

©1989 United Feature Syndicate, Inc. All rights reserved. Printed in the U.S.A.
No part of this book may be reproduced or copied in any form without written permission from
the publisher. GOLDEN, GOLDEN & DESIGN, A GOLDEN BOOK, A GOLDEN LOOK-LOOK
BOOK, and A GOLDEN LITTLE LOOK-LOOK BOOK are trademarks of
Western Publishing Company, Inc. Library of Congress Catalog Card Number: 88-51400
ISBN: 0-307-11866-5/ISBN: 0-307-61866-8 (lib. bdg.)   A B C D E F G H I J K L M

"Aahhh! What a great life," Snoopy said to himself as he ate another cookie. He sat comfortably in a big soft chair in front of the television. "Whoever said a dog's life isn't so terrific has never lived *this* dog's life!"

903631

Just then Charlie Brown walked into the room. "Hi, lazybones," he said.

Snoopy looked surprised. "Lazybones! Me? He couldn't have been calling *me* lazybones," thought Snoopy. "Could he?"

"You've been sitting in that chair too long," Charlie Brown said. "It's time you started watching your health instead of watching TV. You'd better get up, get out, and get in shape, Snoopy!" Charlie Brown turned and jogged out of the room.

Snoopy stood up. "Maybe I have been sitting in this chair too long," he thought. "Maybe Charlie Brown is right. I should go out and get in shape. But first I need something else to eat." Snoopy headed for his supper dish.

Snoopy ate until his stomach was full.
"Now that I've eaten I can start to think
about exercising," Snoopy said. He took a
deep breath and went outside to see what
everybody else was doing.

The first thing Snoopy saw was Charlie Brown jogging. "I guess he meant what he said," thought Snoopy. "Good old Charlie Brown is sure getting in shape. I feel tired just looking at him!"

Snoopy walked on a little bit. Soon he saw
Lucy jumping rope. Lucy called out to
Snoopy, "Come on, dog. Work out!"

Snoopy watched for a minute. "Jumping
rope just isn't my sport," he decided as he
walked away.

Snoopy came to a spot where Linus, Schroeder, and Peppermint Patty were exercising together.

"Hey, Snoopy," grunted Linus. "Try some sit-ups to tighten your stomach muscles."

"Everybody is after me to join the fit crowd," thought Snoopy as he started walking back home.

"I want to get in shape," thought Snoopy. "But I can't do it alone. I need a friend to help me get started. Someone who is in the same shape I am. Someone who might even be in *worse* shape. I know just the friend to call!" Snoopy ran the rest of the way home.

When Snoopy got home, he called his
friend Woodstock on the telephone. "Hello,
Woodstock?" he said. "This is Snoopy. Meet
me outside in ten minutes. We're going to
get in shape."

Woodstock wondered what Snoopy was
talking about, but he agreed to meet him.

"First I'll just jog around the room a little
to loosen up my muscles," Snoopy decided.
He ran around the room for a minute. "This
isn't going to be as easy as I thought,"
Snoopy said to himself.

"Whew!" said Snoopy as he dropped to the floor to rest. "These legs of mine can really go! They just can't go for very long. I guess I'd better save my energy for outside." Snoopy rested for a few minutes. Then he got up and limped out to meet Woodstock.

Woodstock was already outside waiting
for Snoopy.

"Woodstock," said Snoopy, "we're going to
get ourselves into great shape. First we'll do
some jogging. Are you ready?"

Woodstock was ready.

Snoopy and Woodstock started out
jogging next to each other. Soon the little
bird was way ahead of Snoopy. "Stop," yelled
Snoopy. "That's enough jogging for now. My
paws are aching. Everything is aching. Even
my nose is aching," Snoopy complained.
Woodstock wasn't even out of breath.

"Let's play tennis," said Snoopy. He got
his racket and began hitting balls across
the court. Woodstock picked each ball up
and flew with it back to Snoopy.

Soon Snoopy called, "Time out." He was
gasping for breath and sweat was pouring
down his face. "You look a little tired,
Woodstock," Snoopy said. "Let's do
something else."

Woodstock wasn't really tired at all, but if
Snoopy wanted to try another sport, that
was okay with him.

"Why don't we go bowling," Snoopy suggested. "It's nice and cool at the bowling alley." The two friends walked to the bowling alley. Snoopy threw the ball down the alley three times. Each time the ball rolled into the gutter. "Strike three. I'm out," cried Snoopy.

Woodstock gave Snoopy a puzzled look.
"Oh," said Snoopy, looking a little
embarrassed. "I guess I was thinking of
baseball. Let's turn in the bowling ball and
try a sport we understand better.

"Aerobic exercise is exactly what we both need," said Snoopy after putting on a sweatband and a gym shirt. "Breathe in. Breathe out. Stretch those muscles. Breathe in. Breathe out. Are you with me, Woodstock?" called Snoopy between breaths.

Woodstock watched his friend
breathe in and breathe out. He watched
Snoopy touch his toes and stretch his
muscles. Snoopy was really into aerobics.
"Come on, Woodstock," called Snoopy as he
jumped and danced. "Breathe in! Breathe
out!" Woodstock breathed in and breathed
out.

"Whew!" said Snoopy. "That's it for me!"

Snoopy and Woodstock both felt fit but tired. They climbed to the top of Snoopy's doghouse and started to close their eyes. Then Sally came by.

"Well, look at you two lazybones," she said. "Now, that's the life."

"Good grief," said Snoopy, and he fell fast asleep.